Story and pictures by
MARTHA ALEXANDER

Dial Books for Young Readers ● New York

Published by Dial Books for Young Readers
A Division of Penguin Books USA Inc.
375 Hudson Street
New York, New York 10014

Library of Congress Catalog Card Number: 72-134855
Printed in Hong Kong by South China Printing Company (1988) Limited
E   E   AL
7 9 11 13 15 16 14 12 10 8

for my mother and for Sabrina P.

It was the first day of school, and Sabrina was very excited! As the teacher called the names of the children, each one answered, "Here."

When she called Sabrina's name,

everyone turned to look at her.

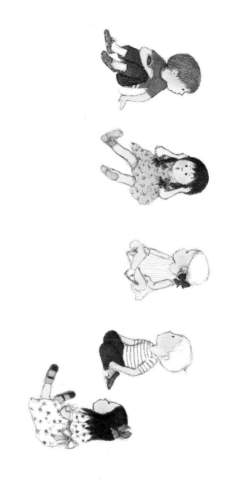

Two girls were whispering, and she heard them say her name.

She couldn't wait for school to be over.
She wasn't having any fun after all.

Her name was not like the others.
There were three Michaels and two
Lisas and two Susans, a David and
an Amy. But not one had a strange
name like Sabrina.

She was so unhappy she wanted to cry.

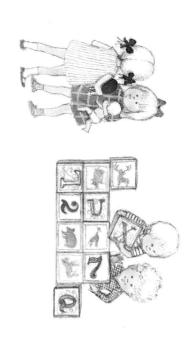

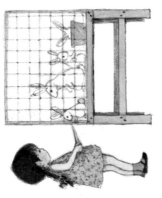

I'll never come back, she thought.
I hate this school and everyone in it.

I'll change my name to Susan or Lisa
and go to another school.

And when I have my birthday party, I'll only invite my new friends.

Sabrina waited until nap time when everyone was asleep.

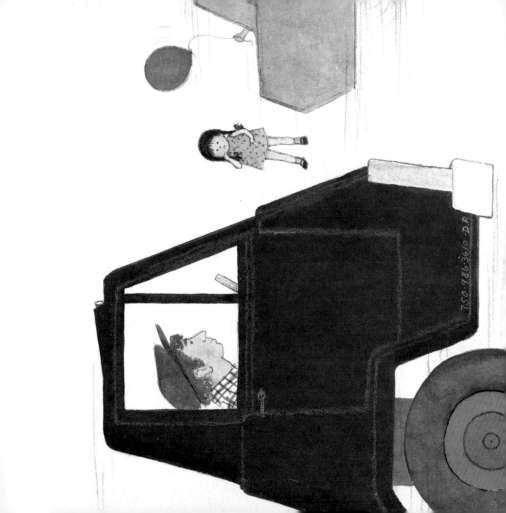

"Oh, Sabrina, we have been looking everywhere for you! What's the matter?"

"Miss Potter, I don't want my name to be Sabrina anymore. I want to be called Susan."

"Then I want to be Sabrina."

"Me too."

"No, Susan, I said it first!"

"Listen, Amy, she chose my name, so I should get hers."

"I want that princess name!"

"No, I want it!"

"Now, girls, why don't we let Sabrina settle this?"

"Well . . ."

"If you give me your name, you can play with my doll."

"If you let me have it, you can ride my new bike."

"Who said I wanted to give my name away?"

"Besides, who would be dumb enough to give away a beautiful name like Sabrina!"